Max Goes to the Space Station

A Science Adventure with Max the Dog

Jeffrey Bennett

illustrated by

Michael Carroll

Editing: Joan Marsh
Design and Production: Mark Stuart Ong, Side By Side Studios

Published in the United States by
Big Kid Science
Boulder, Colorado 80304
www.BigKidScience.com

ISBN-13: 978-1-937548-28-5

Also available in Spanish

Credits
P. 12 Big Kid Box: Diagram from *The Cosmic Perspective* (Pearson Education), adapted from a similar diagram in *Space Station Science* by Marianne Dyson.

Also by Jeffrey Bennett

For children:
- *Max Goes to the Moon*
- *Max Goes to Mars*
- *Max Goes to Jupiter*
- *The Wizard Who Saved the World*

For grownups:
- *On the Cosmic Horizon*
- *Beyond UFOs*
- *Math for Life*
- *What is Relativity?* (2014)

Textbooks:
- *The Cosmic Perspective* series
- *Life in the Universe*
- *Using and Understanding Mathematics*
- *Statistical Reasoning for Everyday Life*

Special Thanks To:

Astronaut Alvin Drew worked closely with the author and artist throughout the development of this book, offering numerous suggestions that made their way into the story line and carefully checking both text and art for technical accuracy with the real International Space Station.

Patricia Tribe also worked closely with the author and artist, and she created (with astronaut Alvin Drew) the *Story Time From Space* program through which this book will be read from orbit aboard the real International Space Station.

The Center for the Advancement of Science in Space (CASIS) is providing logistical support for the *Story Time From Space* program.

Expert Reviewers

Tyson Brown, National Science Teachers Association
Debbie Brown-Biggs, Educational Consultant
B. Alvin Drew, Astronaut
Andrew Fraknoi, Foothill College
Jeff Goldstein, National Center for Earth and Space Science Education
Justin Kugler, CASIS
Susan Lederer, NASA Johnson Space Center
Mark Levy, Educational Consultant
Diane Matthews, CASIS
Cherilynn Morrow, Aspen Global Change Institute
Patricia Tribe, T^2 Science and Math Educational Consultants
Mary Urquhart, UT Dallas
Helen Zentner, Educational Consultant

In Memoriam — Alan Okamoto (1957–2012)

Alan Okamoto illustrated the first two books in the Max Science Adventure series (*Max Goes to the Moon* and *Max Goes to Mars*). He was extraordinarily talented and one of the kindest people you could ever meet. We hope that his work will continue to touch the hearts of children around the world, as he touched the hearts of all those who knew him. To honor Alan's memory, we have painted him into this book as one of the astronauts on pages 16 and 26.

Look for hidden objects in the paintings throughout the book. For hints and other "secrets of the pages," visit www.BigKidScience.com/ISS.

To Children Around the World —

The International Space Station is a real place, orbiting high above our planet, built and operated by thousands of people from all around the world. I hope this story will not only teach you more about space and the International Space Station, but more importantly that it will inspire you to join in the global effort to build a better future for all of us.

Astronaut Alvin Drew works outside the International Space Station.

A Note from the Author

We are living at perhaps the most important turning point in human history. Our science and technology have brought us wonders that our ancestors could scarcely have imagined, but they have also given us power that is too often used for destructive purposes. Our future therefore rests on the hope that all of us can learn to use our power wisely, so that we turn the future only toward the better.

I write books about space exploration because I believe that we're far more likely to succeed in building a better future if we know what that future might look like. In prior books of this series, I've tried to show what we could do for real in the not-too-distant future by sending Max on fictional journeys to the Moon, Mars, and Jupiter. But there is one place in space where humans are already living and working, and that is the International Space Station. Built through the cooperative efforts of people representing virtually every nationality, race, and religion, the International Space Station is a shining example of what humans are capable of when we work together for the common good.

This particular book is actually a "prequel" to *Max Goes to the Moon*, which opens with a parade celebrating Max's trip to the Space Station. This book will tell you how that parade came to be, but its real goals are to educate you about science and the International Space Station, to show you the incredible new perspective that we gain by looking at Earth from above, and to inspire you to make your own contributions to the future of the human race. After all, if we all make our best efforts, it is only a matter of time until our children will travel widely among the planets of our solar system, and our descendants will set sail for the stars.

Reach for the stars!

— Jeffrey Bennett

This is the story of how Max's adventures in space began, with a trip to the International Space Station.

Tori and her family had just arrived at the playground with Max. Tori and her brother ran ahead. Max could barely contain his excitement, but he waited obediently until Tori's dad gave him the OK. Then Max raced to the merry-go-round, where he began circling it and pushing it with his paws.

Soon it was spinning fast. Tori and her brother held on tight. Max hopped on and off, sometimes riding and sometimes pushing it along faster.

Max and Newton

The real Max really did love to play with merry-go-rounds, and in doing so he demonstrated a dog's ability to understand how motion works. Max learned through experience that he could speed up the merry-go-round only if he pushed both down and forward as he ran, not if he pushed straight down.

We humans also learn through experience, but we can do much more. We can take our experiences and use them to discover laws of nature that allow us to understand how things work and to predict future events.

Among the most important laws of nature are the laws of motion and the law of gravity, all published by Sir Isaac Newton in 1687. These laws can be applied not only to merry-go-rounds, but to all types of motion. In fact, scientists and engineers use these laws to figure out exactly how to get a spacecraft into orbit (or beyond) and to predict exactly where the spacecraft will be tomorrow, next week, or next year.

* * *

In case you were wondering: The real Max never went down a slide (and never went into space), but he was once invited to perform his merry-go-round trick on David Letterman's show. Unfortunately, the show crew was unable to set up a merry-go-round on stage, so Max's appearance was cancelled. Watch a video of Max on a merry-go-round at www.BigKidScience.com/maxvideo.

When the merry-go-round finally came to a stop, a woman walked over to Tori. "Your dog is amazing," said the woman. "Does he go down the slide, too?"

"I don't know," replied Tori. "He might if we help him up the ladder."

The woman helped Tori and her dad, and sure enough, Max sailed down the slide.

The woman turned to Tori's dad. "Please call," she said, handing him a business card with a photo of the International Space Station. "I have an idea for your dog."

The International Space Station

The International Space Station is the largest and most complex structure ever assembled in space. Including its solar panels, it spans an area larger than a football field. If it were on the ground, it would weigh about 450 tons.

The International Space Station orbits at an altitude that varies between about 330 and 410 kilometers (205–255 miles) above Earth's surface. It circles our planet at an average speed of about 28,000 kilometers per hour (17,000 miles per hour), which means it goes all the way around our world about every 90 minutes.

The International Space Station is a partnership between the space agencies of the United States, Russia, Canada, Japan, and the European Union, and scientists and engineers from virtually every country in the world have contributed in at least some way. The first module was launched in 1998, and the last major U.S.-built module was delivered in 2011. Delivery and assembly required more than 100 rocket launches, including 37 Space Shuttle missions. (Most of the other launches were Russian rockets.)

Today, the International Space Station is used primarily for scientific research, but it also has secondary roles in promoting education, international cooperation, and the development of space-related industries.

Later that day at home, Max was in the back yard wrestling with a big stick. Tori was inside doing her homework. Her dad was on the phone, talking to the woman who'd given him the business card.

"Really? Are you serious?" he asked. Tori couldn't hear the woman on the other end.

"Well, OK then. When's the launch?"

Tori leapt up. "What did you just say?!" she exclaimed.

First in Space

Have you ever wondered who was the first to ride a rocket into space? In fact, several animals went into space before any people. As the story says, a dog named Laika was the first, launched into orbit on November 3, 1957. The animals who followed her included other dogs, monkeys, mice, and a chimpanzee named Ham.

The first person launched into space was Russian "cosmonaut" Yuri Gagarin, who orbited Earth on April 12, 1961. The first American in space was Alan Shepard, who made a suborbital flight on May 5, 1961, and the first American to orbit Earth was John Glenn on February 20, 1962. The first space walk (going outside a spaceship in a spacesuit) was made by cosmonaut Alexei Leonov on March 18, 1965.

The first woman in space was cosmonaut Valentina Tereshkova, who made her trip on June 16, 1964. The first Hispanic and first person of African descent was Cuba's Arnaldo Tamayo Méndez (September 18, 1980). For Americans, the first woman was Sally Ride, who lifted off in a Space Shuttle on June 18, 1983. The first African American in space was Guy Bluford (August 30, 1983), and the first African American woman was Mae Jemison (September 12, 1992).

There have been many other "firsts" in space, but the best may be yet to come: When will *you* make your first trip into space?

Her dad explained: "The woman we met today represents a wealthy client who loves dogs. The client wants to send a dog to the International Space Station in honor of Laika, the Russian dog who was the first living creature to go into space. She thinks Max is the perfect choice for the trip."

"Oh, I'm not so sure about that," said Tori.

Outside, Max was airborne as he *almost* caught a Frisbee thrown by Tori's brother. Her dad laughed. "It looks like he can do just fine with weightlessness," he assured her.

Is Max Really Weightless When He Jumps?

Tori's dad wasn't kidding when he said the airborne Max was doing "just fine with weightlessness." Most people don't realize it, but you become temporarily weightless every time you jump into the air.

You can understand why by imagining that you are standing on a scale on the edge of a diving platform. The scale reads your weight because gravity makes you push against it, while the platform makes sure the scale stays in place. Now suppose that someone pushes you and the scale off the platform, so you both start falling toward the water. Because you and the scale are both falling — you are in *freefall* — you'll no longer be pushing against the scale and it will therefore read zero. In other words, while you are falling, you will have become weightless!

More generally, you are in freefall whenever there is no ground or anything else for you to push against, even if you are going up (like when you jump up on a trampoline) rather than down. In fact, the only difference between the weightlessness you experience when you jump and the weightlessness of astronauts in the Space Station is that their weightlessness lasts a lot longer — but we'll come back to that story on Page 14.

Astronaut Training

Training for Max was all fun and games, but real astronauts work very hard.

Astronauts use many types of equipment to train. Some machines allow them to experience forces like those they'll feel during launch. They use virtual reality equipment to practice jobs they'll do in space. Airplanes can fly special trajectories that allow passengers to experience a total of a few minutes of weightlessness during a flight. To train for space walks, astronauts wear spacesuits in the Neutral Buoyancy Laboratory, the world's largest indoor swimming pool. It is big enough to hold full-size models of parts of the Space Station, so that the astronauts can float underwater and get a sense of how it will feel to work while floating in space.

Would you like to try some astronaut training for yourself? You can do so by going to Space Camp at the US Space and Rocket Center in Huntsville, Alabama, or to one of several other Space Camps around the world, including Space Camp Canada, Space Camp Turkey, and Space Camp Belgium.

Astronaut Alvin Drew heads down in the Neutral Buoyancy Laboratory.

Max would be going as a space tourist, but he still needed some training.

Tori traveled with him to Houston, where astronauts train at the Johnson Space Center. It was serious business for the humans, who wanted to be sure that Max could withstand the forces of launch and the feeling of weightlessness in orbit.

Max, however, seemed to think it was all fun and games. He swam in the water tank where astronauts train and used machines that simulate different parts of the space experience. He also made many new friends, including Commander Grant, who guided all the training.

Launch day arrived at last. The media had made a big story of a dog going into space, so the launch drew an unusually large crowd to watch it. Tori and her family were there, of course.

To help keep Max calm during the launch, NASA sent Commander Grant along with him. Excitement built as the announcer reached the end of the countdown. "5... 4... 3... 2... 1... Liftoff! We have liftoff of Max the Dog, the first dog to visit the International Space Station!"

Space Tourism

Would you like to take a vacation in space? It may soon be possible, even if you are not an astronaut.

In fact, several wealthy people have already gone into space as "space tourists," though the ticket price (more than $20 million!) is still far too high for the average person. Fortunately, many private companies are working to bring that price down, often in partnership with NASA or other government agencies. History suggests that they will succeed. After all, the first trips between continents were hugely expensive for their times, but today tens of thousands of people fly across the oceans each day.

If the same thing happens with the cost of space flight, then by the time you have your own children, you may be able to take a short vacation in space, or even spend spring break on the Moon. Maybe you'll even bring your dog!

Why So Fast?

To understand why the Space Station goes so fast in its orbit, imagine that you had a really tall tower (as in the diagram below).

If you simply stepped off the tower, gravity would make you fall straight down. If you ran and jumped, you'd move forward as you fell, landing away from the base of the tower. The faster you ran out, the farther you'd go before landing.

Now, imagine that you used a rocket to shoot yourself out of the tower so fast that you went forward just as fast as gravity made you fall. By the time you'd fallen as far as the length of the tower, you'd already have moved so far around Earth that you'd no longer be going down at all! In other words, you'd be in orbit, meaning that your forward speed would always keep you above the ground even as gravity always tried to pull you down.

The required speed for orbit is about 28,000 kilometers per hour at the Space Station's altitude, which is why the Space Station—and any ship docking with it—must orbit Earth at this speed. The required orbital speed becomes gradually slower at higher altitudes.

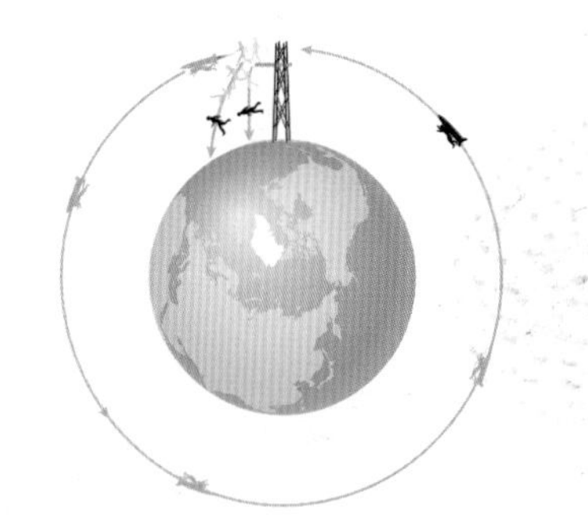

Orbit means going fast enough that your forward speed always keeps you above the ground.

Tori used a video link to talk to Max and Commander Grant as their spaceship headed toward the Space Station. She had lots of questions.

"Aren't you worried about crashing into the Space Station?" she asked Commander Grant. "I heard you are going fast enough to circle the world every 90 minutes!"

"That's true," he replied, "but we don't have to worry about a high-speed collision. Our speed is nearly the same as the Space Station's speed, so for us it will seem that we are approaching it very slowly, even though we are both going very fast in our orbit."

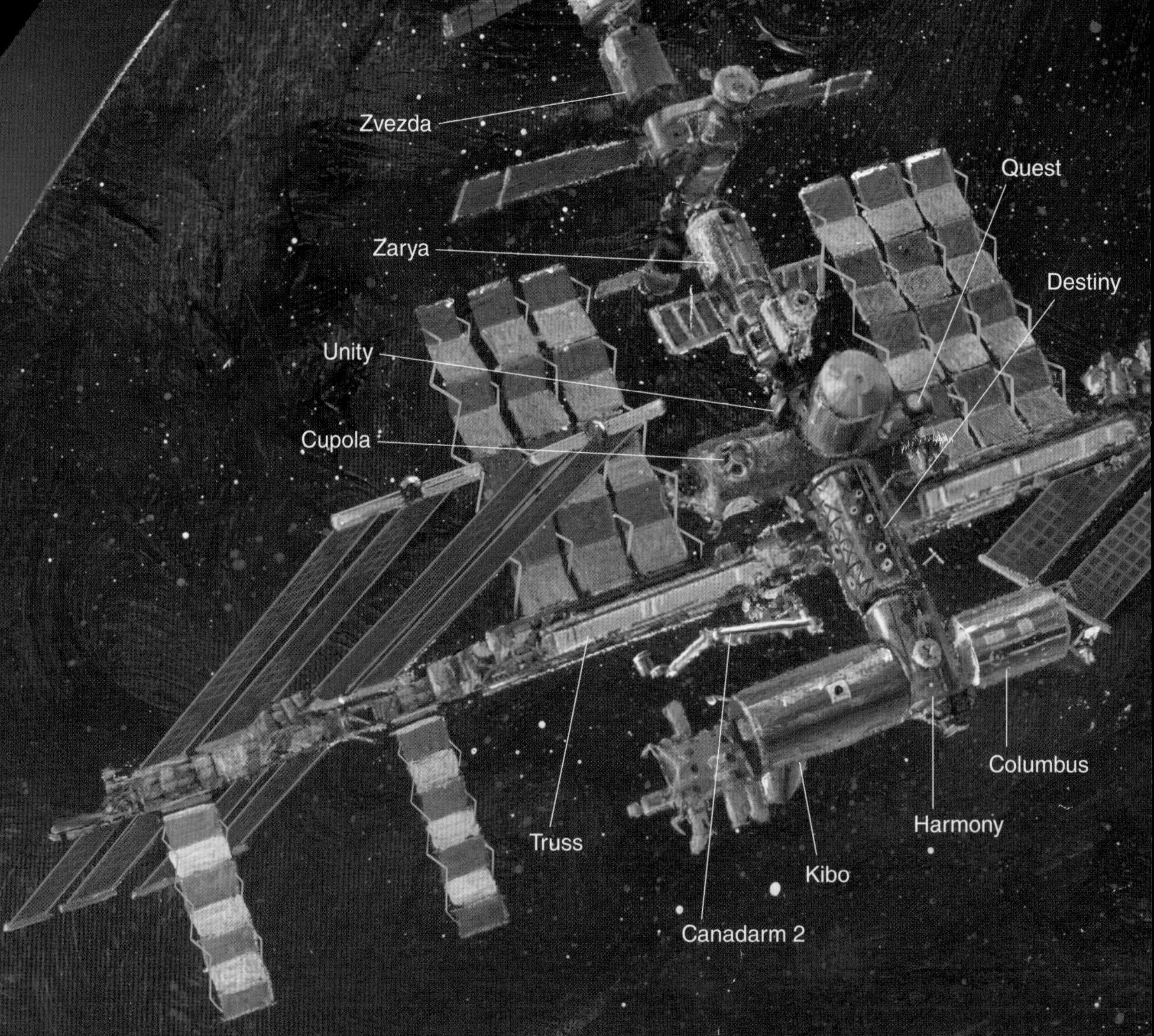

As the spaceship closed in on the Space Station, Tori watched a live video feed showing the view. "Wow!" she said, "it's huge! What do all those different parts do?"

Commander Grant pointed to the various parts as he replied. "The shiny solar panels provide the power," he said. "And all those cylindrical sections are where we live and work. We call them *modules* and each one has a name."

Commander Grant guided the spaceship to a perfect docking with the Space Station. Then Max and Commander Grant floated through the hatch, where they were greeted by the crew members already living there.

Solar panels

Radiators

Getting to Know the International Space Station

The painting on this page shows the International Space Station, with labels for some of its major parts. Here's a little bit about what each one does.

The **truss** is a lattice used to hold all the pieces together.

Solar panels provide power.

Radiators help keep the inside of the Space Station cool.

Zarya was the first module, now used primarily for storage.

Zvezda holds flight computers, the kitchen, sleeping quarters, a toilet, and other vital components for life on the station.

Quest is the airlock through which space walkers enter and exit the Space Station.

Unity connects the Russian and US sections of the Space Station.

Destiny is the US laboratory where astronauts perform science experiments.

Columbus is the European laboratory for conducting science experiments.

Kibo is the Japanese laboratory for science experiments.

Harmony connects the laboratories and contains living quarters.

Canadarm 2 is a robotic crane used to move equipment and space walkers around the outside of the station.

Cupola is the room with windows pictured on the cover of this book.

Many other important components are not labeled, and more may be added in the future.

Things did not go smoothly at first. Max was disoriented by being weightless. He tumbled aimlessly, annoying the crew. Watching on video, Tori asked, "Why are you weightless in space? I thought there's gravity everywhere."

"That's true," replied Commander Grant. "In fact, Earth's gravity holds our Space Station in orbit. We are weightless because we are in what we call *freefall*, and that means we don't feel the gravity.

"What you call weight," he continued, "is really the feel of gravity making you push against the ground or floor. In space, there's no ground for us or our Space Station to push against, so we feel just as you would if you were falling, and that makes us weightless."

Why are Astronauts Weightless?

If you ask why astronauts are weightless in space, a lot of people will try to tell you that "there's no gravity in space." To convince them that this is untrue, just remind them that gravity keeps the Moon in orbit around Earth. The Moon is much farther away than the Space Station (about 1,000 times as far!), so if Earth's gravity is strong enough to hold the Moon in orbit, it's obviously plenty strong at the Space Station's altitude.

The real reason astronauts are weightless is just what Commander Grant and Tori tell us: The astronauts and the Space Station are in freefall, and freefall makes you weightless. Remember (from Page 12) that orbit means moving forward just as fast as gravity pulls you downward, so the astronauts and station continually "fall around" Earth without ever hitting the ground.

More generally, astronauts and spaceships are weightless any time they are traveling through space on a path determined solely by their forward speed and gravity, whether it is Earth's gravity, the Sun's gravity, or the gravity of another world (such as the Moon or a planet). They have weight only when they push against something, such as their own spaceship when its engines are firing, or when they land on another world.

"Wait a minute," said Tori. "Does that mean I can become weightless just by jumping up into the air, since that would mean I don't feel the ground anymore?"

"Exactly," answered Commander Grant. "The only difference is that you are weightless only for the short time until you come back down, while we stay weightless in the Space Station because our high speed keeps us orbiting the Earth."

"Aha!" said Tori. "So that's why you can tumble and twist like gymnasts and divers when they are in the air. It's kind of like you and the Space Station are falling around the world together, which means you feel like a diver who never hits the water!"

Where Does Space Begin?

The International Space Station is obviously in "space" and airplanes obviously are not. So how high do you have to go to change from being "in the air" to being "in space"?

To answer this question, think about what happens as you go higher. If you've ever hiked up a mountain, you know that the air becomes thinner, making it harder to breathe. The air pressure also gets lower. For example, at the altitudes where most airplanes fly, the air pressure is less than 20% of what it is at sea level.

The air keeps getting thinner as you go higher, so that it gradually becomes impossible to breathe and the pressure gradually becomes so low that you need a pressurized spacesuit or spacecraft to survive. The sky also becomes black even in daytime, because as you go higher there is no longer enough air to scatter sunlight across your sky.

Because all these changes are gradual, there's no official definition of where space begins. Still, an altitude of about 100 kilometers is commonly called "the edge of space," because no airplane could ever fly this high.

By the second day, Max was getting used to being weightless, and the crew began to appreciate his playful personality. They especially loved meal time, when they'd toss him food and blobs of water. Sometimes a crew member would give Max a little push so he'd be floating in the right direction for the catch.

The only problem came when they tried to give Max a special steak that his trip sponsor had sent along for him. Max caught it just fine, but then he let it go and began to whimper. Worried, Commander Grant called Tori to see if she knew what was wrong.

Living in Space

Max's food games illustrate some of the things that astronauts deal with when living in space. Water forms little blobs that float, so you can drink by catching them. But don't let them hit a wall — they'll break into many smaller blobs and you'll have a watery mess. Food creates similar challenges, as crumbs will float all over the place.

When it's time to go to sleep, you can't lay down in a bed. Instead, you'll float, so you'd better tether yourself to a wall so you don't bang into anything important. Some astronauts use sleeping bags, and closet-size personal cabins are available. Interestingly, almost everyone sleeps with their arms in front of them when they are weightless.

Perhaps the biggest challenge of daily life is the toilet. It can't have water (because it would float out), and you can't "go" like normal, since everything would float. Instead, a space toilet uses suction to send body waste to special containers, and these are ultimately sent back to Earth for disposal. Oh, and in case you're wondering how Max used the toilet... well, we're going to leave that one to your imagination!

Tori laughed when she heard the problem. "I know it sounds silly," she said, "but he won't eat the steak unless you cut it into small pieces. He doesn't realize how big he is, so he assumes he needs to eat like a small and sensitive dog."

That evening, Tori went outside and caught a glimpse of the Space Station as it flew overhead. "Sweet dreams," she said softly to Max.

Seeing the Space Station

Like Tori does in the story, you can sometimes see the International Space Station as it orbits overhead. You just need to know what you are looking for and when to look for it.

Let's start with what you are looking for. Although the Space Station is pretty big, remember that its orbit keeps it an average of more than 350 kilometers (220 miles) above the ground. At that distance, you won't see any detail with just your eyes. Instead, when it's visible, the Space Station will look much like a bright star, except that it will be moving slowly across your sky, taking between 2 to 5 minutes to go from horizon to horizon.

As for when to look for it: The Space Station shines by reflecting sunlight, so your best chance to see it is either shortly after sunset or shortly before dawn, when your sky is dark but the Space Station hasn't yet gone behind Earth. Moreover, its orbit takes it over different places at different times, so you'll need to know exactly when it will make an evening or pre-dawn pass over your location. You can find apps and web sites that will give you the needed details.

Nighttime made Tori think of another question for Commander Grant. "How do you know when to go to sleep?" she asked. "With the Space Station circling Earth every 90 minutes, it seems like you'd have 45 minutes of daylight and 45 minutes of darkness on every orbit!"

"You are right again," said Commander Grant. "We have very short days and nights. It can be a little strange, but it also means we get to see lots of beautiful sunrises and sunsets. As to our schedules, we still use regular clocks, and we always make sure that everyone gets enough sleep."

Telling Time in Space

On Earth, we set clocks by the Sun. Earth rotates in 24 hours, and we say that the time is around noon when the Sun reaches its high point in your sky. (The exact time of the high point depends on where you live within your time zone and is closer to 1pm when we are using Daylight Saving Time.)

As you probably know, Earth's rotation also means that noon comes at different times in different places. For example, when it is noon for you, it is midnight on the opposite side of Earth. We divide the world into *time zones* so that everyone's clocks read close to noon when the Sun is highest in their sky.

The problem for the Space Station is that, as Tori explains, its high speed means it travels all the way around the world, through day and night, every hour and a half. So how do astronauts set their clocks? In principle, they could choose to use the time for any location on Earth, but for historical reasons they use the time in Greenwich, England, usually called "Greenwich Mean Time (GMT)" or "Universal Coordinated Time (UTC)." In fact, this time is used as a general reference time around the world. If you look up your time zone on the Web, it will state how it differs from Greenwich time. For example, if it says your time zone is "UTC–8," it means your time is 8 hours behind Greenwich time.

Back at home, Tori lay in bed and thought about the work the astronauts do on the Space Station. She knew that the astronauts spend much of their time doing science. They study Earth as they orbit above it, and do experiments to learn how weightlessness affects things like living cells, plants and small animals, the growth of crystals, and chemical reactions. They also do medical research that will help future astronauts on missions to distant worlds.

Tori was soon asleep. That night, she dreamed of being a scientist and astronaut herself, taking trips not only to the Space Station but also to the Moon, Mars, Jupiter, and beyond.

Science on the Space Station

There is a lot of science that is possible on the Space Station but not on Earth. Much of this work involves experiments to learn about the effects of weightlessness or of the airless environment of space. Scientists on Earth design the experiments and astronauts carry them out. Most experiments focus on one of four areas of science:

1. Human health. Future space missions, such as missions to Mars, will require astronauts to live in space for long periods of time. It's therefore important to understand how weightlessness and space affect us, so that we can be sure the astronauts will remain healthy.
2. Materials science. This means such things as learning how different materials react to being in space and how crystals grow when floating weightlessly. This type of research has already led to new manufacturing techniques that can be used on Earth.
3. Biology. In addition to understanding how space and weightlessness affect humans, we also want to know how they affect plants and other living organisms. After all, we'll need plants to recycle air and provide food on long space missions, and biology in space often turns up surprises that are more difficult to study when weight is involved.
4. Combustion science. This means learning such things as how fuels burn, which will help in developing future rockets and manufacturing capabilities.

Tori woke up with excitement, because this was going to be a very special science day. The astronauts were going to begin the next set of student space flight experiments — science experiments designed and built by students just like her! She and her friends were already thinking up ideas, in hopes that they could design an experiment that might be selected one day.

After breakfast, Tori watched the video feed showing the astronauts at work.

Student Spaceflight Experiments

Would you like to build an experiment that will fly on the International Space Station? It really is possible, thanks to the Student Spaceflight Experiments Program (SSEP), run by the National Center for Earth and Space Science Education.

If you'd like to participate, the first step is to learn all the program requirements. After all, this program is real science, so you'll have to make sure your experiment meets requirements for size, safety, materials, cost, and more. You'll also need to make sure that you find ways to include your entire school community, or even your entire school district or region.

If your experiment is selected, you'll build it to fit in a special "mini-laboratory" that will be launched on a rocket to the International Space Station. Once there, astronauts will help carry out your experiment, and you'll get data with all the results so you can analyze them and draw your conclusions.

Why not give it a try? Already, tens of thousands of students have participated in some way in the Student Spaceflight Experiments Program. To learn how you can join them, visit the program web site.

Each experiment was stored in a special "mini-laboratory." The astronauts carefully unpacked each experiment and then started to set it up. Everything seemed to be going very well. But suddenly…

Max began to bark. He had a very loud bark, and the crew was especially surprised because they had never heard him bark before. Max was clearly disturbed by something.

Commander Grant quickly pushed himself toward Max. With worry in his voice, he asked, "What's wrong, Max?"

Studying Earth from Space

It might seem surprising, but some of the most important science done in space is about our very own planet Earth. The reason is that space gives us a broad view of our planet that we just can't get on the ground.

You can see the idea in photographs from space. For example, we can see a hurricane's swirling clouds from above, long before its winds and rain hit land. More generally, the Space Station and other satellites allow us to do what we call "remote sensing," in which special instruments look down at Earth and measure temperatures, wind speeds, ocean currents, and much more. These types of measurements give us a much deeper understanding of how our planet works, and they are important for studying the impacts of human-caused global warming.

All in all, observing Earth from above may be the most important role of the entire space program. Not only does it provide us with science we cannot get otherwise, but it has given us an entirely new appreciation of our blue world.

This NASA image shows Hurricane Irene (2011) photographed from orbit.

Max would not stop barking no matter how much Commander Grant tried to calm him. Then Commander Grant noticed that Max was looking intently in one direction.

Commander Grant instantly realized the problem. The Space Station's cooling system was leaking, which meant that poisonous ammonia gas was getting mixed into the air they breathed. Max and the astronauts would all be killed if they didn't do something quickly. Fortunately, the crew was well-trained in how to stay calm and focused during emergencies.

Danger!

Astronauts are hopeful that the International Space Station will never have an emergency quite as bad as the one described in this story, but there are many dangers when living in space. To begin with, astronauts must always have enough food, water, and air. This means that rockets must be sent regularly to the station with these supplies, and water and air must be recycled as much as possible.

The station is pressurized, since there is no air outside it, and complex systems are needed to keep the inside environment safe and comfortable. The electronics and people in the station produce a lot of heat, which is why the station needs the cooling system that leads to the emergency in this story. But this is only one of many systems that could pose danger if they leaked or failed.

Another great danger is posed by "space junk" — orbiting debris that could potentially puncture the station, causing damage or allowing air to escape to space. Radiation from the Sun can also create danger, especially during "solar storms." The station has protected areas where astronauts can take shelter at such times.

What if a major emergency really occurred? Just in case, the station always has Russian *Soyuz* capsules docked to it, which the astronauts could use to return to Earth in an emergency evacuation.

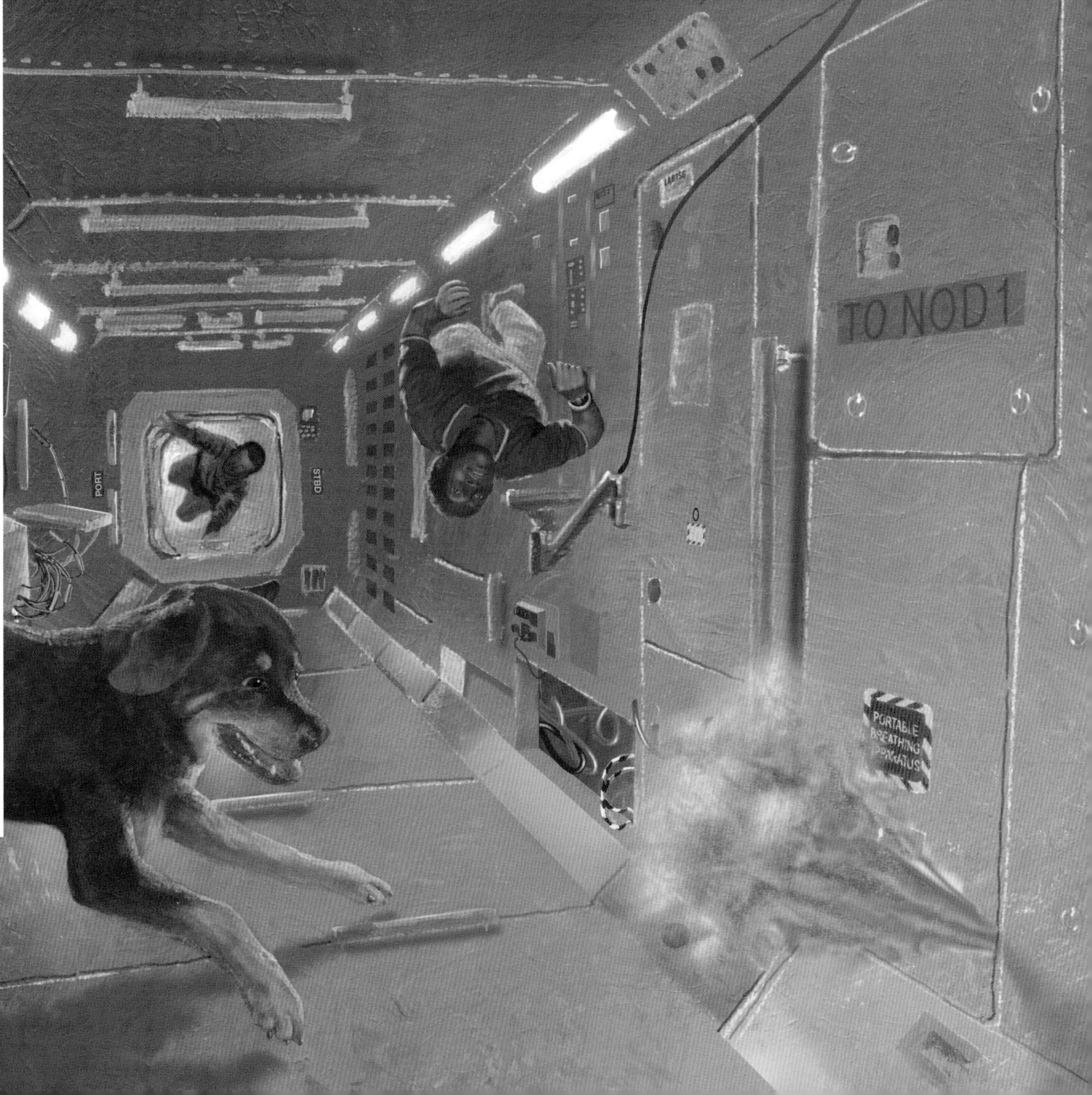

Commander Grant quickly determined that the leak would have to be repaired from outside. His crewmates helped him get ready, and soon he had his spacesuit on and tools in hand. He went out through the airlock, using miniature jets on his spacesuit to get close to the cooling system. Then he used handles on the outside of the Space Station to anchor himself in place while he worked.

In truth, the repair was very difficult. But you would have never known that from hearing Commander Grant as he worked. If he was ever worried at all, he never showed it. Soon, he was back inside, problem solved.

EVA

When astronauts go outside in a spacesuit, we sometimes say that they are on a "space walk." However, since you obviously can't walk while floating weightlessly in space, the more formal term is "extravehicular activity," or EVA.

It's not easy to work during EVA. Spacesuits must provide all your life support systems while you are outside, so they are more like small personal spaceships than pieces of clothing. This means you have large gloves, which can make it difficult to use your hands.

There are also challenges to getting around. If you simply pushed off from one part of the station, you'd find yourself floating away into space. Astronauts therefore use tethers to keep themselves attached to the station, and handholds on the station exterior allow the astronauts to pull themselves along. They can also fire small jets on their spacesuits to move around, which can be especially important if a tether becomes unhooked. Sometimes, astronauts hitch a ride on one of the station's robotic arms, with someone inside moving them to wherever they need to go.

Despite the challenges, astronauts who've been on EVA say it is one of the most amazing experiences of their lives. After all, they are floating outside the Space Station, looking down at Earth as they orbit. You couldn't ask for a more spectacular view.

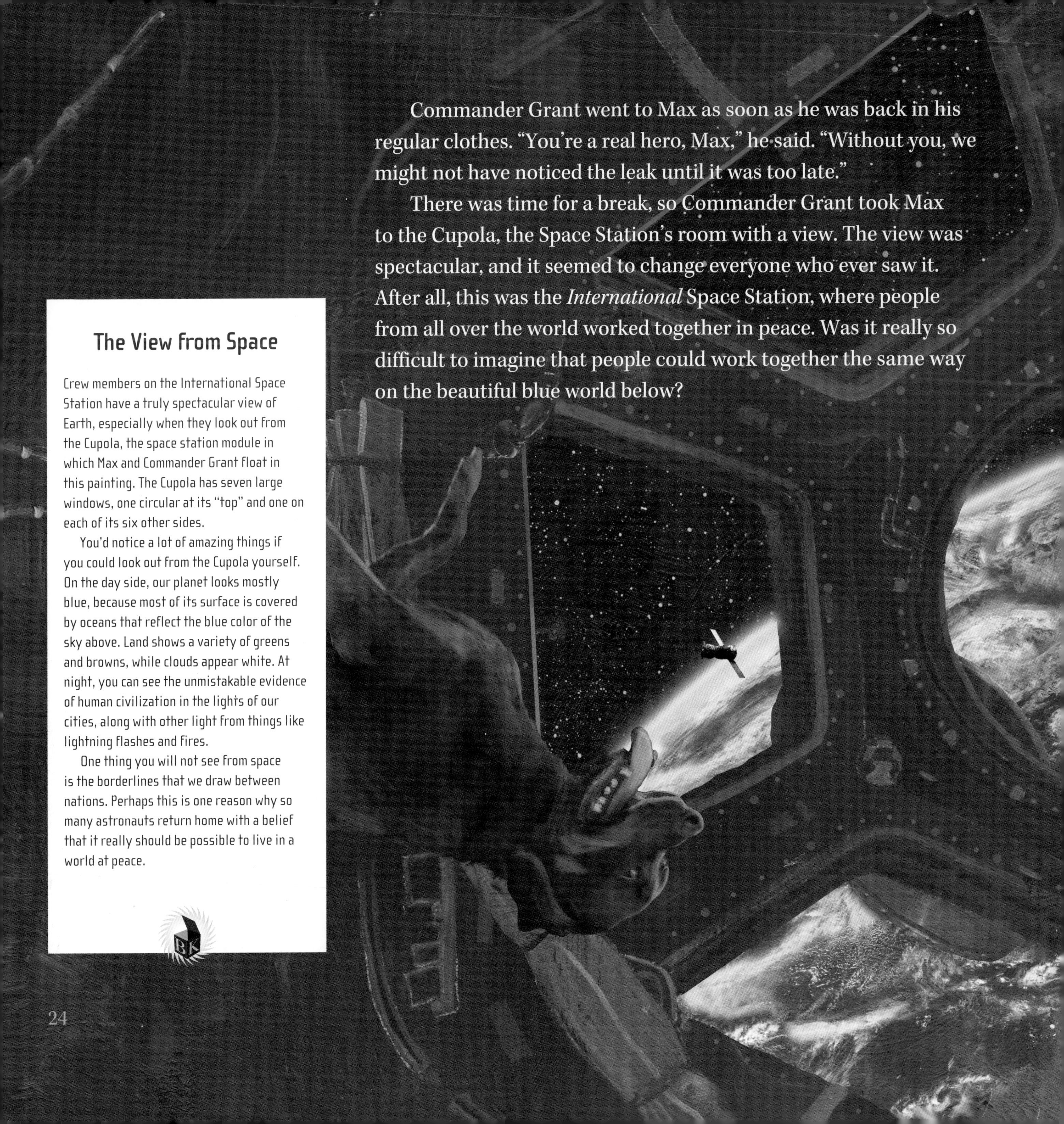

Commander Grant went to Max as soon as he was back in his regular clothes. "You're a real hero, Max," he said. "Without you, we might not have noticed the leak until it was too late."

There was time for a break, so Commander Grant took Max to the Cupola, the Space Station's room with a view. The view was spectacular, and it seemed to change everyone who ever saw it. After all, this was the *International* Space Station, where people from all over the world worked together in peace. Was it really so difficult to imagine that people could work together the same way on the beautiful blue world below?

The View from Space

Crew members on the International Space Station have a truly spectacular view of Earth, especially when they look out from the Cupola, the space station module in which Max and Commander Grant float in this painting. The Cupola has seven large windows, one circular at its "top" and one on each of its six other sides.

You'd notice a lot of amazing things if you could look out from the Cupola yourself. On the day side, our planet looks mostly blue, because most of its surface is covered by oceans that reflect the blue color of the sky above. Land shows a variety of greens and browns, while clouds appear white. At night, you can see the unmistakable evidence of human civilization in the lights of our cities, along with other light from things like lightning flashes and fires.

One thing you will not see from space is the borderlines that we draw between nations. Perhaps this is one reason why so many astronauts return home with a belief that it really should be possible to live in a world at peace.

For a little while, Max and Commander Grant just enjoyed watching out the windows as they circled around the world beneath them. Finally, Commander Grant knew it was time to broadcast a report to people back home on Earth.

He began by telling everyone how Max had saved the astronauts' lives. Then, knowing that many school children were watching and listening, he pulled out a book. "It's time for our Story Time From Space," he began.

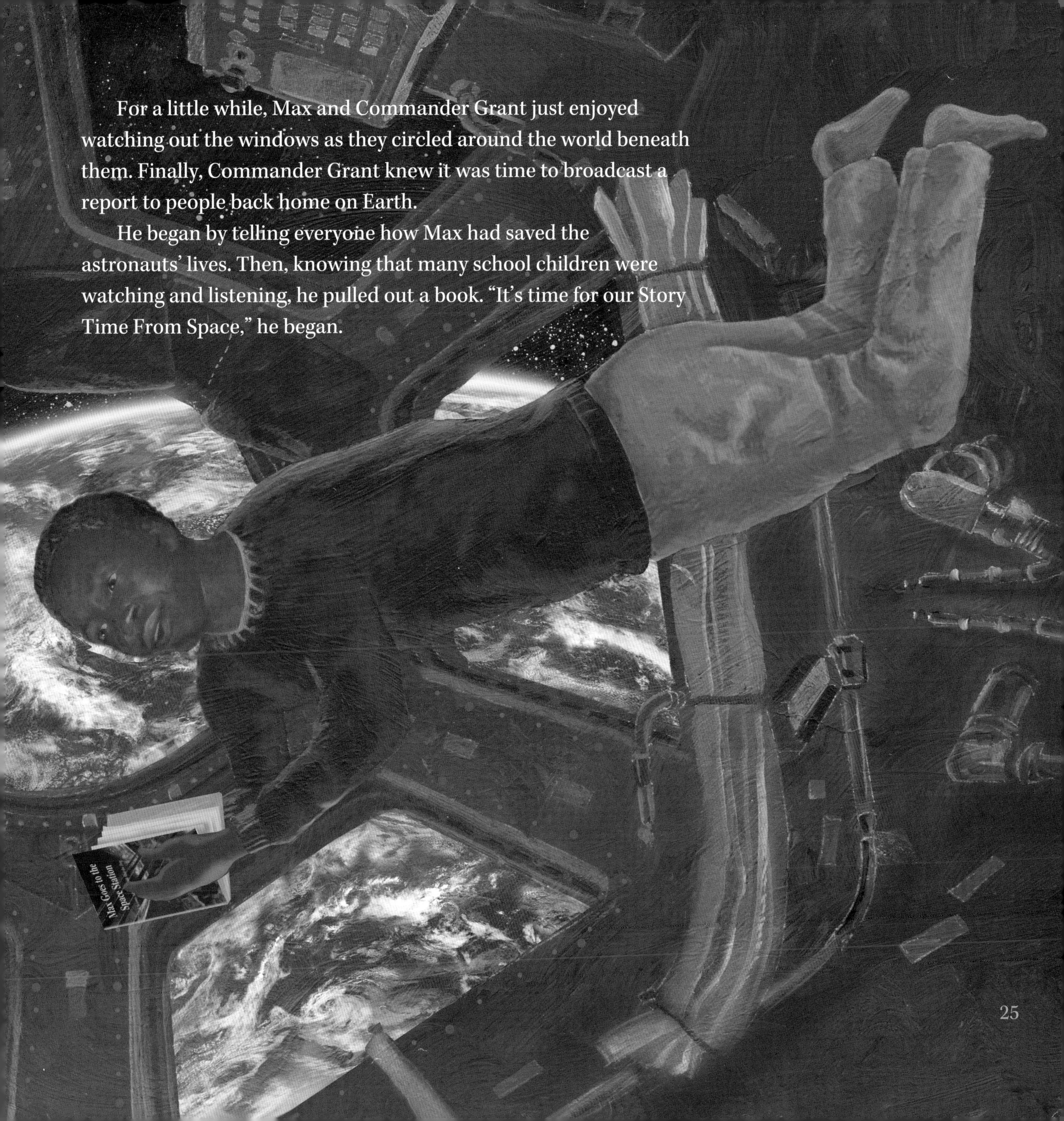

The rest of Max's visit passed uneventfully for him, though the crew was busy working as always. Just a week after his arrival, it was time for Max to go home.

Most of the other astronauts would remain aboard the Space Station for months, so they all gathered around to say goodbye to Max. They had all come to love him, and several of them suggested that it would be a good idea to send a dog on future space missions. Finally, they all posed for one last space photo with Max.

Astronauts

Have you ever wondered what *astronaut* actually means? If we break the word into pieces, *astro* comes from a Greek word for "star" and *naut* comes from the Greek word for "sailor." So taken literally, an astronaut is a "sailor of the stars."

There are other names for astronauts. For example, Russian astronauts are called cosmonauts, which means "sailors of the universe." Chinese astronauts are sometimes called taikonauts, which combines the Chinese word for space ("taikong") with the Greek word for "sailor."

Although only the United States, Russia, and China have launched people into space, astronauts have come from nearly every country in Europe and from many other countries, including Canada, Japan, Mexico, Brazil, South Korea, India, South Africa, Israel, Saudi Arabia, Malaysia, Afghanistan, and more.

Astronauts also come from a wide range of careers, including pilots, doctors, scientists, engineers, and teachers. But no matter where they come from or what jobs they hold on Earth, astronauts work together in space, and all return home to their families with the same joy and the same new perspectives on our home planet. It's an experience that will gradually become available to more and more people. Perhaps someday you, too, will become a sailor of the stars.

Max was soon back on Earth. His legs were a bit wobbly after a week of weightlessness, but he still had a big lick for Tori when she ran over to greet him.

Max's trip had been everything anyone could have hoped. He'd become a hero, he'd honored dogs in space, and he'd gained the love and admiration not only of the astronauts but of people all over the world. Most importantly, his trip inspired children everywhere to work harder in school, and to dream of their own trips to the Space Station and far beyond.

With the journey complete, Max and Tori returned home, where Tori and her friends planned a big parade for Max. It would be a spectacular event.

Our Future in Space

The International Space Station is an important outpost in space, but ultimately its greatest purpose will probably come through its role as a stepping stone to even greater things. By proving that it is possible for humans to live in space for long periods of time, it is showing that we are ready to return to the Moon, go on to Mars, and continue beyond.

Of course, some people wonder why we should bother exploring space, or whether it is worth the cost. Different people have different answers to these questions, but here's the opinion of the team that produced this book:

We are living at a turning point in human history. Today, we face many serious global problems, including problems caused by war and hatred, and problems that we create through pollution and global warming. Our future depends on solving these problems, and our best chance of solving them will come if children everywhere are inspired to dream, to work hard, and to build a better future. There's no better source of this inspiration than space exploration, which reminds us that everything is possible. If we put our minds to it and all work together, we'll not only solve the problems of today, but we'll create a future that will someday take human beings throughout the solar system, and onward to the stars.

Meanwhile, high above, the International Space Station continues to circle our world. There is no sound to hear in space, so it circles silently. Completing an orbit every hour and a half, it reminds us that the planet we all share is remarkably small, and the narrow blue band of our atmosphere on the horizon reminds us that a thin layer of air is all that protects us from the harsh environment of space.

Thanks to Max, many more people now understand what it all means. Working in space may someday help us learn to live on other worlds, but its greatest value is in the way it teaches us the importance of taking care of our own world. After all, no matter how far we travel in the future, Earth will always be our home planet, and if we don't take good care of our home, no one else will.

Suggested Activities

Astronaut Biography (Grades 1–4)
Have you ever thought about being an astronaut? There have been hundreds of astronauts and cosmonauts in space, and some of them probably were much like you when they were young.

- Search the Web for pictures of astronauts, and find one who might have looked much like you when he or she was young.
- Write a short biography of your astronaut. Be sure to learn what the astronaut studied in school and what jobs your astronaut held before becoming an astronaut.
- Present your biography as an oral report to family, friends, or school. Be sure you've learned enough about your astronaut to answer questions that may not be covered in your written report.

Build a Space Station (Grades 3–8)
Create your own Space Station, which you'll build as 3-D art.

- Visit NASA's web site to learn more about the International Space Station and all its components. Then make a list of the crucial components that you'll want your own Space Station to have. Include a brief description of the purpose of each item on your list.
- Draw a sketch to show how your Space Station will be assembled. Then come up with a plan for making a three-dimensional model of your station.
- Build your model, and show it off to friends, family, and teachers as you describe how your station works. Don't forget to give it a name!

Write Your Own Max Science Adventure (Grades 3–8)
Max has now been to the Space Station, the Moon, Mars, and Jupiter in Big Kid Science books. Where would *you* like to send Max next? Choose a destination, then write and illustrate a story of Max's adventures.

- Your story should be exciting and include an opportunity for Max to be a hero, but remember that he's a real dog, not a talking dog.
- Be sure that your story includes some real science. You could even include your own "Big Kid Boxes" on the sides of pages, or a Question and Answer on each page that teaches about the science.
- Classes, schools, or districts could consider sponsoring a Max Science Adventure Writing Contest. Some places have already done this, and one district winner was actually published as a Big Kid Science book! (The book is *Max's Ice Age Adventure*, written by Logan Weinman, who was a third grader at the time.)

Earth Observation (Grades 5–8)
As discussed in this book, one of the most important scientific roles of the Space Station is in studying Earth. Many other orbiting satellites also study Earth.

- Do a little Web research about the kinds of things that space observations help us learn about Earth. Then choose one type of observation to research in more depth. Examples might include studying storms from space, measuring ocean currents from space, learning about global warming from space. There are many other possibilities as well.
- Once you've chosen a type of observation, find at least 10 images of Earth from space that show this observation type. Compile your images into a journal, along with brief written descriptions of what each image shows.
- Add an introduction to your journal that explains the type of observation you've studied, why it is important, and what it has helped us learn about Earth.

Elevator Science (Grades 6–8)

If you can find a tall building with a fast elevator, you can explore the way weight changes under different conditions by taking a small bathroom scale into the elevator with you. You'll need to ride up and down for a while, so be prepared for some funny looks from others who get on the elevator with you. Note: This experiment works best if you can take the elevator many floors without stopping.

- Ride the elevator up and down a couple of times. You should notice six distinct stages in its motion:
  1. As it begins to go up, the elevator accelerates, gradually increasing its upward speed.
  2. Soon, the elevator settles into a steady (constant speed) upward motion.
  3. As it nears the top (or a floor on which it is stopping), the elevator will slow down until it comes to a stop.
  4. When you head back down, at first the elevator will accelerate downward, going faster and faster until it reaches a steady speed.
  5. It will maintain the steady speed for a while.
  6. As it nears the bottom (or a floor on which it is stopping), the elevator slows to a stop.
- Once you can feel the various stages, use your bathroom scale to see what happens to your weight. During which stages does the scale show you to be heavier than your normal weight? Which stages show you to be lighter? Which stages show your normal weight? (Hint: Of the six stages, you should find that you are heavier than normal in two, lighter than normal in two, and normal in two.)
- Based on what you've learned, discuss what would happen if the elevator cable were to break. What would the scale show in that case? How would this demonstrate that freefall makes you weightless like an astronaut?

More Activities

We are hoping to develop many more classroom activities to go with this and other books of the Max Science Adventure Series. You can find updates on the latest activity set and other related resources for education by visiting our web site:

www.BigKidScience.com

Story Time From Space

Are you ready for an exciting new program that combines literature with science and math education? If so, then *Story Time From Space* is for you.

Conceived by Educational Consultant Patricia Tribe and Astronaut Alvin Drew, the *Story Time From Space* program began with Astronaut Drew reading *Max Goes to the Moon* from orbit during STS-133, the final mission of the Space Shuttle Discovery. You can watch the video by going to www.BigKidScience.com/max_in_space. Tribe and Drew then teamed up with the Center for the Advancement of Science in Space (CASIS) to expand the program with readings from orbit on the International Space Station. This book, *Max Goes to the Space Station*, came about when that team decided it would be the perfect choice for the first book to be read from the International Space Station. They approached the author with the idea, and the fact that you are reading this book shows that he agreed to write it.

Of course, *Story Time From Space* is meant to be much more than just a series of readings. Some of the goals of the program include:

- Engaging children's imaginations and interest in space exploration, science and math concepts, and literature.
- Creating a variety of media to build upon children's enthusiasm for *Story Time From Space* books, including planetarium shows (a *Max Goes to the Moon* planetarium show is already available) and television or on-line educational programming.
- Providing educators with lesson plans and supporting materials for integrating *Story Time From Space* selections into school curricula, aligned with current math, science, and literacy standards.
- Offering wide, international, and low-cost or free access to *Story Time From Space* videos and supporting materials.

You can learn more about *Story Time From Space* by visiting
www.StoryTimeFromSpace.com

EN VIVO
DESDE LA
EEI